Cinderella at the Ball

Modern Curriculum Press
BEGINNING
TO
READ
Series

CINDERELLA
at the Ball

Margaret Hillert

Illustrated by Janet LaSalle

MODERN CURRICULUM PRESS
Cleveland • Toronto

Library of Congress Catalog Card Number: 75-85952

ISBN 0-8136-5532- 3 (paperback)
ISBN 0-8136-5032-1 (hardbound)

6   7   8   9   10

92 91 90 89

Come to the ball!
Come to the ball!

Oh, Mother, Mother.

We can go to the ball.

We two can go.

A ball is fun.

Come here, you.

Run, run, run.

You can help.

We want you to help.

7

Look here, Mother.

Here we go.

Away, away.

I want to come, too.

A ball is fun.

You!
You go to the ball!
Oh, not you.
You look funny.
And you can not come.

11

I can not go.
I look funny.
Oh my, oh my.

Look up, little one.

Look up and see me.

I can help you.

You can go, too.

See here.

I can make something for you.

One, two, three!

Here it is.

15

And look here.

Here is something big and orange.

You can go to the ball in it.

Here it is.

It is for you.

Go in, go in.

Look, look.

One little one.

Two little ones.

Three little ones.

See here.

One big one.

Two big ones.

Three big ones.

Away you go.
Away, little one.
Away to the ball.
A ball is fun.

20

Here I go.
Up, up, up.
Up to the ball.

Oh my, oh my.

It is fun here.

Fun for you and me.

Oh, look.

Oh, oh, oh.

Here I go.

Run, run, run.

26

Where is the little one?

Find the little one for me.

Go and look.

Go, go.

Where is the little one?

Come here.

Come here.

We want to find you.

Not you.
Not you.
It is not you.
Go away.
Go away.

Here you are, little one.

I like you.

Come with me to my house.

Margaret Hillert, author and poet, has written many books for young readers. She is a former first-grade teacher and lives in Birmingham, Michigan.

CINDERELLA AT THE BALL

The popular fairy tale of Cinderella is retold in 44 preprimer words.

Word List

5	come	6	is	11	not	14	for
	to		fun		funny		three
	the	7	here		and		it
	ball		you	12	my	16	big
6	oh		run	13	up		orange
	mother		help		little		in
	we		want		one(s)	27	where
	can	8	look		see		find
	go		away		me	31	are
	two	9	I	14	make		with
	a		too		something		house